Tadpoles

Dad's Van

First published in 2008 by
Franklin Watts
338 Euston Road
London
NW1 3BH

Franklin Watts Australia
Level 17/207 Kent Street
Sydney
NSW 2000

Text © Mick Gowar 2008
Illustration © Rory Walker 2008

A CIP catalogue record for this book is available
from the British Library.

ISBN 978 0 7496 7964 4 (hbk)
ISBN 978 0 7496 7970 5 (pbk)

The author and publisher
would like to thank Robert
Kearney for permission to use
the photograph on page 4 (top).

Series Editor: Jackie Hamley
Editor: Melanie Palmer
Series Advisor: Dr Hilary Minns
Series Designer: Peter Scoulding

Printed in China

Franklin Watts is a division of
Hachette Children's Books,
an Hachette Livre UK company.

Dad's Van

by Mick Gowar

Illustrated by Rory Walker

W
FRANKLIN WATTS
LONDON • SYDNEY

Mick Gowar

"I've always wanted to go on holiday in a camper van. I could take my whole family, including all the pets – but I wouldn't want the van to break down!"

Rory Walker

"This story reminds me of my dad's old, custard-coloured car. It had big white wings too, but it didn't break down as often as this van!"

It was holiday time.

But the van would not start.

"I'll have to push,"
said Dad.

"I'll help," said Mum.

"We'll help," said
Emma and Sam.

"Woof!" said Alfie.
"Miaow!" said Dina.

"Squawk!" said Pedro.
"Squeak!" said Peanut.

"It's started!" said Dad.

"Who's driving?"
asked Mum.
"Not me," said Dad.

"Not us," said
Emma and Sam.

"STOP!"

everybody cried.

19

The van stopped ...
and wouldn't go.

"We'll have to push,"
said Dad.

But Mum said, "No,
I've got a better idea!"

23

Notes for adults

TADPOLES are structured to provide support for newly independent readers. The stories may also be used by adults for sharing with young children.

Starting to read alone can be daunting. **TADPOLES** help by providing visual support and repeating words and phrases. These books will both develop confidence and encourage reading and rereading for pleasure.

If you are reading this book with a child, here are a few suggestions:

1. Make reading fun! Choose a time to read when you and the child are relaxed and have time to share the story.
2. Talk about the story before you start reading. Look at the cover and the blurb. What might the story be about? Why might the child like it?
3. Encourage the child to reread the story, and to retell the story in their own words, using the illustrations to remind them what has happened.
4. Discuss the story and see if the child can relate it to their own experience, or perhaps compare it to another story they know.
5. Give praise! Remember that small mistakes need not always be corrected.